THE KITCHEN MADONNA

THE
Kitchen Madonna

RUMER GODDEN

Illustrated by Carol Barker

THE VIKING PRESS   NEW YORK

For Elizabeth Rumer

THE KITCHEN MADONNA

THE CHILDREN did not like it that Marta was unhappy.

"Well, she chose to come, didn't she?" said Janet.

"Haven't you ever chosen to do something and not liked it at all?" asked Father, and Janet had to admit she had. Gregory had not. "But then Greg hardly ever does anything," Janet could have said. Gregory was a quiet boy, always first in his class at school but oddly out of things at home. "He puts himself out of things," Janet would have said and Mother complained, "Gregory keeps himself to himself."

Then Marta had come to help in the house—"Help! She *is* the house," Gregory might have said—and from the first he had taken an interest in her, which was strange because he had taken none at all in the much younger Danish Tove and French Babette who had preceded her. "But Tove was so good at games; she could play with you," said Mother. Gregory did not like games. "And Babette was so gay." Babette's gaiety had made Gregory more quiet than ever.

Marta neither played games nor was gay. She was from the Polish Ukraine, "And no wonder she's sad," said Mother. "Think of the history of her country." But Gregory thought Marta's sadness had nothing to do with her country, it was of now; though Marta was in late middle age and Gregory was a small boy, he too sometimes felt that brooding unhappiness, especially at twilight, "When Mother is still out," he might have said, only he preferred to keep that thought to himself.

"He never hugs you as Janet does," and Mother sighed. "He's so wrapped up in himself that sometimes I wonder if he has a heart—and he's so possessive." It was true that Gregory was almost fiercely possessive; no one, except Janet now and then if she asked permission, was allowed into his Loft; no one must touch his things—his ship picture, his books, his birthday watch, or his cat Rootle. Rootle was called Rootle because Gregory had found him as a starving kitten rootling in a dustbin; he was Gregory's, not Father's or Mother's or Janet's. But, from the first day Marta came, Gregory let her stroke Rootle, even feed him and pick him up.

Marta was a boon to Mother. "She's the best help we have ever had," said Mother. Mother and Father, Mr. and Mrs. Thomas, were both busy architects, which made hard work for Mother, who had the children to look after and the house to run besides the office; often she was kept late, or else had to go away to inspect a house or site and then she worried. Marta had only been with them three months but already Mother was looking less harried. Marta was tireless, clean, and a beautiful cook, "Though she does give you children rather too rich and spicy foods." But, "Borsch and goulash, yummy!" said Janet and, "Stay with us forever," she begged. If Marta wished, she could stay; she had not come for a year like Babette and Tove and, "We're so tired of changes," said Gregory. Ever since he could remember, the changes had been continuous; as soon as they got used to one person she went and another came —"One after the other," Gregory could have said.

To Gregory, the important thing about Marta was that she was always there. When they came down in the morning, Marta was in the kitchen making coffee and toast, putting out bowls of cereal, heating rolls, setting the table with honey and milk. When they came in from school she had their tea ready on the kitchen table and to Gregory it was inexpressibly lovely to come home knowing the house would be lit and welcoming instead of dark, forsaken, with a note telling them to go next door. When they went to bed they knew the house was safe because Marta was downstairs in the kitchen getting dinner ready. She put her own plate on a newspaper at one end of the kitchen table. "Marta! You must have a tablecloth," cried Mother when she discovered this but, "I like newspaper. I try read new words," said Marta. When she had washed up, she went quietly up to bed in her room next to Gregory's and Janet's bedrooms.

"But don't you want to go out?" asked Mother.

"I go out," Marta answered in her slow way. After years in England she still spoke English haltingly. "I go to the shop, take knitting in the Gardens. Where else?" asked Marta. She did go to church on Sundays but this was early in the morning before the family was up. It was peaceful and, "Steady," said Gregory, not continually upsetting as it had been with Tove and Babette, who were always wanting to go out, so that complicated arrangements had to be made for Gregory and Janet and they felt "like incubi," said Gregory, using one of his special words. Mrs. Peebles, the daily woman, had to come in and sit with them, which made them feel they were babies, or he and Janet were sent to spend the evening with friends—"Not my friends," said Gregory; or else Teresina, the Italian cook next door, kept an eye on them—and when they were alone in the big house, it felt even bigger and more lonely. Holidays were worse, because then it went on all day. "Always being fobbed off on people," said Gregory. It was not only this; Tove and Babette had brought their friends to the house. "We were *invaded*," said Gregory; sometimes he used odd expressions for a nine-year-old boy. "Invaded."

"But it's nice to have people," Mother told him. Gregory did not think it nice. With Tove and Babette the house had not felt like the Thomases' own; with Marta it did, "Because there's no one here but us," said

Gregory. Without thinking, he included Marta when he said "us." Marta, it appeared, did not want friends. The old lady she had worked for in the country had died. "Me there twenty-two years," said Marta.

Twenty-two years! "That's ages," said Janet. Long, long before they were born, more than twice as long.

"You must have liked it, to stay so long," said Gregory jealously.

"No, not like," said Marta.

"Then why did you stay?" demanded Janet.

"Old lady, ill. She need Marta," said Marta, as if that settled it.

"We need you too," said Janet, and the whole of Gregory longed to say that as well: "We need you. Stay with us forever." But he was tongue-tied and Mother filled him with dread when she sighed and said, "I'm afraid it's too lonely for Marta."

"Make it less lonely," said Gregory. He meant it as a plea, but it sounded like a growl and Mother did not answer. Besides, how could she make it less lonely? Marta was so heavy and slow, her clothes so old-fashioned, that the other maids and cooks and mother's helps in the Square laughed at her. It seemed too that she did not want to make friends, not even with genial Teresina, who talked enough for two; when Marta saw Teresina she popped back into the kitchen like a rabbit into its hole. Gregory did the same.

"It's no good forcing her," said Mother, and soon it

was settled that when the family was out, Marta was content to be with Rootle.

Marta and Rootle had both suffered from the world; Marta, Mother said, had been a refugee from her village, driven out by soldiers, and had never seen her mother and father or any of her people again. Rootle had been driven out too, but unlike Marta, he was skinny, perhaps because he had been so starved. Marta limped from a wound—"They shoot at me," said Marta—and Rootle's tabby coat had a bald spot where, "Perhaps someone threw boiling water at him," said Mother. "Oh! Oh!" cried Janet, and Gregory picked up Rootle and held him tightly. One of Rootle's ears, which must have been cuffed or injured, had grown crooked. Marta, though, thought Rootle beautiful, as Gregory did, and she used to talk to him: "*Moja kicia. Kicia,* my kitty. Kitty," she would say, though Rootle was by no means a kitten. "*Moja kicia,*" and Rootle would purr. Sometimes he answered with a "miaow" but there was something wrong with Rootle's miaow; when he opened his mouth, only a ghost of a sound came out, hoarse and stifled, as if those days of being out in the cold and wet had hurt his throat. "But now," said Marta, "he has beautiful big home, *moja kicia.*"

The home was big; Gregory's Loft was in the roof and had the house cistern in its corner; the cistern made gurgling noises that seemed company for him when he worked. On the next floor were the children's two bedrooms—Janet's was the old nursery—with Marta's bedroom next to them. The floor below was Mother and Father's, with their bedroom, dressing room, and two workrooms; below that again was the drawing room and the dining room; in the basement Marta had her own sitting room next to the kitchen, but she always sat in the kitchen. "Why, Marta? In your room there's television and a comfortable chair."

"I like kitchen," said Marta. "In my home," she told the children, "only one room, and that room kitchen."

"One room for everyone to sit in?" asked Janet.

"Sit, cook, eat, wash, sleep, everythings," said Marta.

"In a kitchen like this?" asked Janet, marveling. And she asked, "Where were the beds?"

"No like this," said Marta. "No cooker, only big oven, big, big, big! On top of oven big bed all childrens sleep."

"On top of the *oven?*" asked Gregory and Janet together. "But wasn't it too hot?" asked Gregory. "Didn't they get burnt?"

"Oven have many, many bricks all round. Bricks keep it not too hot; nice, warm," said Marta. "I sleep there when I little. One side of room, big wooden bed, Father and Mother sleep; mattress straw and there is big pillow, many, many pillow, beautiful pillow." Marta's green eyes were shining. "White linen cases my mother spin, all embroidered red. Other side room, wood table, chairs, stools to sit and eat. Only one window, so little that room always little dark, but fire it shine, pans they shine. Floor is earth," said Marta and suddenly, as if

15

she were dazed, she looked round the expensive London kitchen with its white paint, white tiles, pale blue Formica, white enamel, silver chromium. "Not like this," said Marta. "Not at all." Mother had planned the kitchen herself. "It's beautiful, isn't it?" she had said when she showed it to Marta, but Marta had said nothing, in a silence which was curiously like Gregory's.

Since Marta came, the kitchen was not quite as beautiful. She brought in a sagging old armchair she had found in the attic lumber room next to Gregory's Loft.

"Why that old chair, Marta?"

"I like," said Marta.

Rootle's basket appeared—"Doesn't Gregory mind?" asked Mother again—but he did not seem to mind. A row of plants stood in odd saucers and glass jars on the window sill with a wooden box planted with parsley and chives, while strings of onions hung on a nail by the door. Marta's work basket spilled socks over one of the cabinets and there were always clothes rolled in a damp towel ready for ironing. "I'm afraid Marta's not very tidy," said Mother, but Gregory and Janet, especially Gregory, liked the kitchen far better now. It was warm and cozier. "It's getting filled," Gregory said one day but Marta shook her head. "It empty."

Sometimes, in her blunt way, Marta said such things to Gregory. She could say them to him; Janet, like Mother, would have been a little indignant, but Gregory only opened his gray eyes wide behind his spectacles, showing that he was surprised and interested.

"How can it be empty when it's full of things? More things since you came, Marta."

"It empty," insisted Marta. "Things not fill—here," and she clasped her hands over the bib of her apron. "Kitchen, it feel empty...." She might have said more but just then Janet came bouncing in and Marta turned quickly to the pan that was bubbling on the stove.

Gregory never forgot things—"He's like a small elephant," said Father—and a week later, while Gregory, Janet, and Marta were having tea in the kitchen, he took his chance. Marta had made a wonderful cake-tart of apricots glazed with jam and they had eaten and drunk and laughed. Marta's usually sallow cheeks were quite red; her eyes, which were often so dull, were bright. There was not a trace of sadness in the air until Gregory put down his cup and asked in his small, quiet way, "What did you have in your kitchen, Marta, that we don't have in ours?"

For a moment Marta did not speak. Gregory thought she was going to retreat into her silence, and in a voice that Mother had not heard, and Janet seldom had— "Only when he speaks to Rootle," Janet could have said—a voice that coaxed like a beguiling little flute, he said, "Tell us, please tell us, Marta."

Marta twisted her hands in her apron and her cheeks flushed deeper red. Then, "You have no 'good place,'" said Marta.

"No good.... What do you mean?" Janet was beginning when Gregory kicked her under the table.

"What is a 'good place,' Marta?"

"In my home, Ukrainian home," said Marta, "we make a good place. In the corner, there," and she pointed to an angle of the room. "A place on top of cupboard, perhaps, or perhaps on shelf. Little place but it holy because we keep there Our Lady and Holy Child."

"A statue?" asked Janet.

"Not statue."

"A picture then?"

"Not picture." Marta struggled to find words. "Like picture but more beautiful. They in our churches too. Pictures, but prickled with gold," said Marta in a rush.

"*Prickled?*"

"She means crusted," said Gregory.

"Crusted," agreed Marta and the *r* sounded rich. "With gold and stones, pearls, rubies . . . ."

"*Real* ones?" asked Janet incredulously.

"Sometimes real, sometimes no. In many churches real," said Marta. "In homes, poor homes, not pearls and rubies. This!" and she went to her work basket and brought out a box. In it were beads, big and little, pale yellow, deeper yellow, and a yellow that was almost brown.

"Amber," said Gregory at once. Gregory knew about stones, jewels, and semiprecious stones; he loved to pore over them in the Geological Museum and liked to say their names aloud: "Sapphire, diamond, emerald, ruby. Onyx, lapis lazuli, carnelian, tourmaline."

"Yes, amber," said Marta and again the *r* rolled. " Rub

it warm and it smell good," said Marta. "They find by the river near my home."

"And do they put amber on the pictures?"

"Yes, to make necklace and decorations. They make embroidery on clothes."

"*Clothes* on a picture?"

"Yes, beautiful," said Marta, rapt away. "The mantle, velvet perhaps, the robe silk. You can feel with your finger," said Marta. "And in front of picture, every day we put vase flowers and a little litted lamp—lamp glass red like ruby too. The lamp shine. All day we see. Kitchen dark, but lamp and picture shine. They faces shine, Mother, Baby; they make happy, warm; everywhere you go, they eyes, they look at you. They look...." Marta looked round and once more saw the Thomas kitchen; the glow left her face and she put her head down among the teacups and wept.

Janet was shocked into silence—she had not seen a grown person cry—but presently Gregory said, as if he had just worked it out, "I know what she means. She means they had a sort of icon."

On Marta's head the skimpy hair was drawn tightly back into a little knob with ugly black hairpins skewered into its dull mouse-color; Marta's pale earlobes were pierced with small gold rings and the worn creases of her neck showed above the carefully turned-down collar. Gregory's heart suddenly swelled with an unfamiliar feeling so that he wanted to cry too, as he had wanted to cry when he found Rootle in the dustbin. He put out his hand and stiffly patted Marta's shoulder—Gregory, who avoided touching anyone. "Don't cry, Marta," he said. "*I* will get you an icon."

"Where are you going?" asked Mother.

"To the Museum."

Mother thought Gregory meant the Geological or the Natural History Museum, where he often went on Saturday mornings. Both were in Kensington, their own part of London. Gregory loved the museums. He made drawings there of stones and crystals, of fossils and skeletons, and brought them back to store in his Loft, tracing more drawings out of books, collecting and labeling them. "But what will you do with them?" asked Janet, who longed to do something with everything. But Gregory did not answer; he only continued to store away.

"So much goes into Gregory," said Mother with a sigh, to Father. "Nothing ever comes out. Just the opposite to Janet."

No brother and sister could have been more different. Janet was pretty, a well-grown little girl, plump, with dimples, lively brown eyes, gold-brown curls. "A cherub," said Marta. Gregory, though older, was smaller, and pale, with thin legs and knobbed knees and strangely large hands with long fingers. "Clever hands," said Mother. His face was small and pale, too, while his big gray eyes were made bigger by dark-rimmed spectacles. When Gregory sat working in his Loft, his face knotted with thought, his hair ruffled, his eyes peering through his spectacles, he looked like an old professor.

Museums are the natural haunt of old professors, but this morning Gregory did not mean the Natural History Museum nor the Geological; he meant the British Museum. One of the few people Gregory ever spoke to, outside the house, was the underkeeper in the fossil room at the Natural History Museum and he had said, "Icons? You'll have to go to the British Museum for those."

"The British Museum," Gregory told Janet. "That's a long way off."

He asked Father to help him look it up on the map of London that Tove and Babette had used. "The British Museum is in Bloomsbury, near Bloomsbury Square," said Father. "Why do you want to know?"

"One day I'll go there," said Gregory. He did not tell Father that the day was this very Saturday. He had worked out the buses they must take—as quite a small boy, "Seven or eight," said Gregory, he had taught himself the London bus routes. The Museum seemed halfway across London and, "We shall have to change buses," he told Janet. "The fares will be expensive but we have plenty of money."

"Yes," said Janet sadly.

When Gregory chose, he could make Janet do anything he wanted and now he had taken all her pocket money. "We have thirty-five shillings between us," he said, "which is more than I hoped. Thirty-five shillings. Then we have threepence of mine and nine pennies of yours." He added, "You can keep your pennies."

"But I want to keep my shillings," protested Janet. "I'm saving up for a pony."

"You mustn't be selfish," said Gregory—he who was always scolded for being selfish.

"If you told Mother, she would buy Marta an icon," argued Janet. "You know she would. Why can't we tell her?"

"You know why."

"It was only Marta who made us promise."

"She isn't *only* Marta."

On that afternoon, when Gregory had patted her, Marta had lifted her head, put back her hair, sniffed loudly, and dried her tears on her napkin. "More than twenty-two years," said Marta. "Twenty-two years I away from my home and never think of it. Now . . . it is talking to children," said Marta. "I not talk so much; it bad." And she said, "You must give me deep promise," (she meant solemn). "Your mother so good to me," said Marta. "Your father give so much money. Marta not ungrateful." The r rolled indignantly at the very idea. "Never! Never! Never! I should *die*," said Marta with vehemence, "if they think that. You—kind boy," she said to Gregory. "Perhaps one day, God, He send Marta a picture."

But Gregory had made up his mind. "God won't give

her that picture, nor Mother, nor Father. I shall," said Gregory.

Gregory was right: the bus was horribly expensive, even though, being under fourteen, they were half-fares. It was a long, long way and, "What time shall we get back?" asked Janet.

"We haven't got there yet," said Gregory, but he was beginning to realize that a Saturday morning was not time enough. Even when they reached the Museum it would take time to find the icons. Gregory knew how big the Natural History and Geological Museums were; the British Museum must be even bigger—enormous, thought Gregory. What time *can* we get back? he wondered.

When they left the bus, even with the map on which Father had shown him the way, they took a wrong turning, and had to ask—"*Twice,*" said Janet. She said it feelingly because Gregory made her ask; he would never speak to anyone if he could help it, but when at last they arrived at the Museum with its great courtyard and climbed the stone steps to the pillared entrance and were in the echoing hall, she refused to ask. Museums were Gregory's territory and she put herself out of the way behind a huge marble statue while Gregory went up to the uniformed man at the desk.

Janet would have said, "Please, where is the icon room?" But when Gregory was forced to speak, he did so clearly and grandly. "Where do you keep your icons?" he asked.

"Are those icons?" asked Janet.

After a long time of wandering, through rooms and galleries, up flights of stone stairs, a keeper had shown them some glass cases in a corner of a large room. "Are *those* icons?"

"I suppose so," said Gregory. There was a card in one case lettered: *Icon panel, 12½ inches. Late 16th century. Moscow school.* There were other cards but the icons were not in the least like Marta's description. To the children's eyes they were rather dull and angular paintings on thick wood, some large and some small, painted and burnished with gold. There were several of the Madonna and Child—what Janet called "Jesus-Marys"; there was Christ on the cross, or his head against gold rays, while some had saints in long robes. The backgrounds of some were gorgeous, red-gold, the color of sunsets, and the robes and sandals and embroideries were painted in fine detail; some of the colors glowed but most were "Smokey," Janet said with distaste. One was silvered all over, just showing the faces and hands; one small Madonna had a cloak and a robe of turquoise enamel but, "Where is the velvet?" asked Janet. "Where are the rubies and pearls? Where is the amber?"

When Janet was disappointed her voice rang out, and a gentleman who was studying a case of miniature jade bottles through an eyeglass looked up. He had glanced at the children once or twice, perhaps amused at the way Gregory stood in front of each icon, gazing at it, his nose almost pressed to the glass. Now the gentleman came over to them. "Don't you think they're beautiful?" he asked.

"No," said Janet and she said again, "Where are the jewels?"

"You mean the clothes and halos are not decorated in silver or gold?" he asked.

"Yes, sir," said Gregory, as formally as if he were at school.

"They're nearly all plain painting," complained Janet. "And why are they so dark?"

"Well, when these paintings were finished," said the gentleman, "they were given a coating of oil and that absorbs the dust and incense. These are old icons, early Greek and Russian; after centuries of worship naturally the paintings grew dark, but that adds to their interest."

Janet did not think so.

"The bright colors are there underneath," the gentleman assured her and he said seriously, "An icon is more than a painting. It is meant to be a link between earth and heaven, a window opening onto sacred things. That's how people looked at them."

Gregory thought he understood. That was how Marta's had felt to her.

"Come and look here," said the gentleman and he led the children to a special case. "Our Lady of Konev," he said. "She has been loved for more than four hundred years. Look at her embroidered cloak."

"But it *isn't* embroidered," said Janet. "That's just it."

"You don't want paintings to be ornamented, young lady." The gentleman sounded severe.

"We do want them to be ornamented," said Janet, so flatly that Gregory had to mouth at her, "You're being rude."

"I'm not. He is," Janet mouthed back. "Trying to make us like what we don't like," she muttered. "Interfering."

But Gregory was interested in what the gentleman had said about the window onto sacred things and, ashamed of Janet, he said, "You see, it was a jeweled icon we were looking for, sir."

"I don't think many were jeweled," said the gentleman.

"Marta said they were," said Janet.

"Some were enameled; Fabergé, for instance, did a fine example."

"Fa-ber-gé?" asked Gregory.

"He was a famous jeweler. His icon is exquisite."

"Where could we see it?"

"I don't think you could; it belongs to the Duke of Norfolk, but there may be others. I should ask a jeweler if I were you."

"A *jeweler?*"

"Yes, Rostov's, off Regent Street, in Panton Place, on the right side as you go up from Piccadilly, specialize

in icons," said the gentleman. "They might help you—
if you must have ornamentation."

"We must," said Janet, and Gregory mouthed again,
"Shut up!" but to the gentleman he said politely,
"Please, sir, could you write that name down?"

The gentleman took out a silver pencil and a card and
wrote on it and gave it to Gregory. It seemed as if he
would make one more attempt to persuade them of the
beauty of the old icons, but Gregory hastily said, "Thank
you," while Janet slipped behind the cases.

"For goodness sake," said Gregory as they scurried
down the gallery, "do you have to be so rude?"

"I wasn't rude."

"You were." And they started to bicker.

"My legs ache," said Janet on the stairs, and in the
hall she rebelled. "I won't go to that jewelers now. I'm
tired and I'm hungry. I want to go ho-me."

"Little softie," said Gregory.

"I'm not a softie."

"Pestering nuisance."

"I'm not a nuisance. You are."

The quarrel was settled for them as a clock chimed
twice. "Two o'clock! It can't be." But it was and they
looked at one another in consternation. "My goodness!
What will Mother say?" asked Janet.

"Extremely, *extremely* naughty," said Mother.
Gregory and Janet had not arrived home until four

o'clock; in his worry Gregory had got them onto a bus going the wrong way, which nearly doubled the journey, and then they had had a long wait at the bus stop until the right bus came along.

"Naughty, deceitful, and thoughtless," said Mother. "Marta was half out of her mind with worry when you didn't come back for lunch. I had a rush of work at the office and had to leave it when she telephoned me there. You know perfectly well you're not allowed to go off without saying where you are going."

Mother was really angry. Gregory's pocket money was stopped for two weeks and they were both sent to bed. "I don't care," said Janet. "My legs still ache." Gregory did not care either. He had the card and the address the gentleman had written: *Rostov, Court Jewelers, 9 Panton Place, Regent Street.* Court Jewelers! Even the words seemed to glitter. "I expect they make crowns," he told Janet, and he conned over the words the gentleman had said. Like an elephant, Gregory did not forget things, and like a parrot, he could remember what people said, word by word—"*If* he is interested," said Mother. He was deeply interested now. "Fabergé did a fine example." He repeated that over and over again: "Fabergé did a fine example." "I shall go to Rostov's next Saturday," he told Janet before he fell asleep.

In the morning, though, Father gave Gregory a good talking to. "London is a big city," he said. "Bigger than you think, and easy to get lost in. You must keep to the part you know; our Square, these streets and the Crescent, the High Street, the Gardens, and the Park. Nine and seven years old is too young to go exploring. It's not fair to Marta, who is responsible for you, and you, as the elder, are responsible for Janet. There is to be no more going off on your own. Are you listening, Gregory?" Father must have caught a faraway look on Gregory's face. "Our Square, the streets around it, and the Park. Nowhere else, Gregory, do you hear me?" asked Father sharply.

"Yes, Father." Gregory had heard and wished he had not. When he came out of Father's room he looked thoughtful and unhappy. Then he sighed and said, "I'm afraid I shall have to be disobedient." "Why?" asked Janet, and Gregory made one of his old-fashioned remarks. "There is no other course open to me; but you needn't be," he said, and when Saturday came, he told Janet to stay with Marta.

"Why?"

"Because I'm going to get into trouble."

"If you get into trouble I don't see why I shouldn't," said Janet, and to all Gregory's arguments she would only say, "I'm coming."

They found Rostov's. It was not really far on a number fourteen bus. They got off at Piccadilly and walked up Regent Street until Gregory caught sight of a sign that said *Panton Place*. Rostov's was on the corner, a big shop with a facade that seemed to be made of dark-gray marble. The windows were small, set deep in the wall, lined with cream-yellow velvet and laced with crisscross gilt bars—"So that no one can smash them," said Gregory, impressed. "Sapphires, emeralds, diamonds," he breathed, gazing at the windows, and though it had begun to rain he stayed a long time gloating over the brooches and necklaces and rings.

"They haven't any price on them," said Janet.

"That's queer." There was no sign of an icon.

"Do you think they really sell them?" she asked.

"The Museum gentleman said so," said Gregory. "He said they specialized." But when he came to the shop door Gregory quailed. It was not like the door of any of the shops in their familiar High Street, set open or swinging cheerfully to and fro; nor were there people going in and out, no women with shopping bags or baskets on wheels or babies in perambulators. The door was of plate glass with a crest, and firmly shut. It was a minute or two before Gergory gathered up enough courage to push it open. Then he and Janet jumped; sitting on a stool just inside was a man in uniform.

"He was a doorman, a kind of keeper-guard," Gregory told Janet afterward.

"A guard, as if they didn't want people to come in," said Janet. It seemed to her a very queer shop.

The doorman got up as they came hesitatingly in. "What do you want, son?"

Gregory did not answer. With Janet pressed close

beside him he stood on a deep crimson carpet. Gregory blinked in the brilliance of light. The shop seemed to spread away on all sides, wall after wall lined with lit cases, glass counters lit too, and all filled with sparkling things. Several men in dark suits, their hair sleek and shining in the light, stood behind the counters. One was talking to a lady; she seemed the only customer in the shop; the rest were simply standing. It was so quiet that above the murmur of the lady's and gentleman's voices the children could hear clocks ticking, innumerable clocks. The shop and the quiet seemed vast.

"Let's go," whispered Janet, but now Gregory was not afraid. This was Rostov's just as he had dreamed; the doorman, when he came to look at him, was not very different from the keepers in the museums—and Gregory did not like being called "son." He stood his ground.

"What do you two want?" asked the man again.

"We want," said Gregory, "to see the owner of this shop." His voice, in its clearness and grandeur, reached all around the room, even to where an older man with white hair was writing at a desk at the back. He looked up.

"The owner, eh?" The big doorman looked down at Gregory with an amusement that nettled him.

"Yes. The owner or one of his men." And Gregory, though Janet jibbed like a frightened little calf, walked up to a counter. Janet followed and stood by the glass case, her eyes growing rounder as she looked at the things inside; when she pressed the glass case with her fingers it was warm. She was so surprised she whispered, "Greg, the glass is hot!"

"Yes?" asked the young man behind the counter. "Yes?"

Gregory was going to speak when Janet, being Janet, spoiled everything. She looked up at the young man and asked in an awed voice, "Do you sell crowns?" "But you said they might," whispered Janet as Gregory's elbow drove sharply into her ribs. "*You* said it."

"I know I did, but not here."

A ripple of laughter had run around among the men; then the young man leaned forward and spoke to Janet in the voice grown people use when they speak to little children—very little children, thought Gregory, scalding—"Crowns? Why, yes. For princesses and fairy queens."

Janet's pink face went pinker, but Gregory turned scarlet and then white, which meant he had lost his temper. "We didn't come here to be laughed at," he said.

Gregory was not four feet tall, but there was dignity in his anger and the way he spoke, and the white-haired man got up from his desk and joined the young man behind the counter. "That will do, Mr. Needham," he said, and he asked Gregory, "What did you come for?" There was not a hint of laughter in his voice.

"I was told," said Gregory, still haughty, "that you sell icons."

"We do, but what kind of icons are you interested in?"

"Not Greek or Russian," said Gregory. "At least, not early Greek or Russian. Later, ornamented icons," said Gregory, and he asked, "Have you any examples of Fabergé?"

"Fabergé?" The man's eyebrows went up; he exchanged glances with Mr. Needham, who openly stared. Then, "We haven't a Fabergé, I'm sorry to say," said the older man, and ordering Mr. Needham as Gregory would have ordered Janet, he said, "Show the young gentleman what we have."

Mr. Needham led the way across the room and opened a glass wall case. There the icons were; after the Museum the children recognized them instantly, though most were brighter, their colors more clear. Three, on the top shelf, were painted of Madonnas and saints; one had baby angels looking out of clouds; another, gold doors that made it like a small shrine; some were dim, but alone on one shelf was an icon of the Mother and Child that riveted Gregory's attention at once.

"Look," he whispered to Janet. "Look." The Mother had a gold crown with, behind it, a circle of stars; the Baby, nestling against her, had a smaller crown. The cloak was blue and studded with silver and in her hand the Mother held a silver ball banded with pinhead red

stones. "It's an orb, "Gregory whispered to Janet. "You remember, when Father took us to see the Crown Jewels we saw the Queen's orb."

"Are the stones rubies?" whispered Janet. She was sure they were rubies but, "Garnets more likely," said Gregory. They gazed and gazed until Gregory said aloud, "That's the one," and told Mr. Needham, "I should like to look at that icon, please."

"You can look at it on the shelf," said Mr. Needham.

"I need to look at it close," said Gregory.

Once again, "Mr. Needham," said the older man and, reluctantly, Mr. Needham spread a square of black velvet on the nearest counter, lifted out the icon, and laid it in front of Gregory. Janet crowded up to see but Mr. Needham kept his hands on each side of it as if he were afraid the children might touch it. Gregory hardly saw the hands; his eyes were all for the icon, searching out every detail.

"It hasn't many jewels," said Janet. "Would Marta like it?"

"Who could help liking it?" Gregory answered, almost absently: so this was what an icon could be like. His eyes went from it to the one with the angels in the clouds, the one with gold doors; none was as beautiful. "This is *the* one," said Gregory.

How was he to know that Janet, the little silly, would take that as being settled? Before he could stop her she had seized his purse out of his hand. "We have spent a lot on buses," she told Mr. Needham, "but we have more than thirty shillings left. Does this icon cost more than that?"

"It costs four hundred and thirty-eight guineas," said Mr. Needham, and again that ripple of laughter ran around the shop.

Gregory did not know how he got outside; he only remembered that there was a buzzing in his ears as he dragged Janet across the crimson carpet and that the shop and its lights seemed to swim around him. "Wait a minute, boy," he heard the older man say, and the doorman laid a hand on Gregory's shoulder, but Gregory shook him off, wrenched open the door, pulled Janet through it, and slammed it shut.

In the street he walked so fast he did not look where he was going and Janet had to trot to keep up with him. "Idiot! Silly idiot," said Gregory, but Janet had no idea what she had done. Her face looked bewildered as she trotted, the rain wetting her hair. She held the purse out toward him; he took it and thrust it out of sight. Thirty shillings. No wonder they had laughed! But it wasn't Janet's fault, he thought. It was mine for going into a shop like that. How could *I* have been so silly? Yet, as he asked that, he remembered the beauty of the Mother's face, the stars around her, the red stones in the orb, the deep-blue of the cloak and he slackened his pace. At least I have seen it, thought Gregory; then the tone of Mr. Needham's voice as he said, "Four hundred and thirty-eight guineas," came back to Gregory so that again he was scalded with shame. I didn't know *anything* could cost so much, he thought, except great pictures of course. He knew pictures could cost thousands and thousands of pounds, but the icon was so little. No wonder they had laughed. He was conscious too of his shabby school raincoat, glistening with rain; of his school cap that he kicked around—"Are you surprised that it looks dusty and frayed?" Mother often said; of his wrinkled socks and scuffed walking shoes. Janet did not look neat either; her coat was shorter than her dress, her hair was rough and her socks were coming down. We ought to have dressed, he thought, dressed properly to go to a shop like that. I ought to have thought. "Fool!" he muttered. "Fool! Fool!" He meant himself, not Janet, but she did not know that. "Greg," she said piteously, "please Greg. It's raining *very* hard."

It was. Janet's hair was beginning to look streaked— she was not even wearing a beret—and as she spoke a drop ran off the end of her snub nose and she shivered. Even when Gregory was cross he was a careful brother and now he looked down the small dark street they were in, up it, and across the way. Then, "There's a church," he said. "Anyone can go into a church. Quick, run in there."

The church was dark too, made darker by the rain, but when they had shaken the drops out of their eyes and stamped their feet to let water squelch out of their shoes, they saw they were only in the porch. "It's got a shop," whispered Janet. "Nonsense," said Gregory. "Churches don't have shops." But at one side there was a sort of shop, full of statues and books and candlesticks. Beyond, in the church itself, they could see a vaulted roof and pillars, and as they walked timidly into it, they saw gold after gold glow, made by candles burning in candlestands all along the walls. The glow was warm, inviting after the gloomy morning outside and they stood looking until Janet pulled Gregory's sleeve. "Look, that's what Marta told us about," she said. "Little lights in red lamps."

In front of a statue two lights burned in small glasses. "Ruby-red," said Gregory but Janet had disappeared. Gregory turned irritably to look for her but in a moment she was back. "Greg," she said, "they have those lamps in the shop." Gregory came to look and Janet was right. The lamps were just as Marta had described them, a glass lamp, deep-red or sapphire-blue in a silvered holder; in each was a round wax light with a wick, like a big nightlight. "Let's buy one for Marta," whispered Janet and she said, "*They* couldn't cost guineas."

There was a notice that read, *If you want something from the repository*—"What a funny name for a shop"—*please ring the bell.* Janet rang and almost at once a small, bent woman in a blue apron came. "Please, how much are those?" asked Janet, pointing to the lamps. They were four shillings and sixpence each. "We can do that," said Gregory. As Janet had seen the lamp first, Gregory let her choose, "Only you must choose a red," he said, and a ruby-red one, with its light, was wrapped in newspaper. Gregory carefully paid out four shillings and six-

pence. "Now we have only one pound, six shillings, and
a few pennies left," he said. "We have spent so much
on fares and it will be another eightpence today. "Yes,
fourpence each way," said Janet and she sighed. "We
can't buy an icon for twenty-six shillings." Indeed it
seemed they could not buy any kind of icon and, "What
use is a lamp without one?" asked Gregory.

All the same the finding of the lamp cheered the day.
He carefully wrapped the shillings and the pennies in
the pound note, put them in his purse, and put that in
his pocket.

It was still deluging outside, and to pass the time,
Gregory and Janet began to walk around the church,
which seemed to have a great many altars where candles
burned on stands. There were several people praying—
"Now, in the middle of the morning," whispered
Gregory—and the children walked on tiptoe until
Gregory suddenly stopped, his fingers digging into
Janet's arm. Hanging against a pillar was a picture, "Or
not a picture," whispered Janet. It was a Madonna and
Child, a Jesus-Mary, in a heavy painted frame, but both
Mother and Child stood out of the picture—"Because
they are dressed," whispered Gregory—dressed as Marta
had described them in cloth and gold. The crowns were
gold lace, carefully cut; the veil and cloak were blue-
edged with silver and stuck with sequins and beads that
glittered. The Mother's robe was red, patterned with
silver, and the Child's small robe was red too, covered
with silver and beads. *Our Lady of Czestochowa, Queen*

of Poland, said a notice under the picture. "That's near Marta's country," said Gregory. "Poland and the Ukraine are almost the same." Below the picture, candles threw a gold light up so that the faces were lit and shadowed, as if they were real, thought Gregory. "Their eyes do look at you," whispered Janet and then she said, "It's Marta's icon."

In her excitement she had raised her voice and, "Hush!" said Gregory. Then he whispered, "It's not an icon." He stepped closer to look. "We were wrong. It wasn't an icon Marta wanted, it was a dressed-up picture." He looked at the picture more and more carefully. "Their clothes are cut out like paper dolls' clothes," he told Janet and, "I could make that," said Gregory.

"But you don't make things," Janet objected. "You never did."

"Only because I didn't want to," said Gregory and gazing at the picture, he began to plan. "I shall need paste," he said. "We must find out the best kind, and pieces of cloth, red and blue and dark-blue." Then, looking at the picture even more closely, he asked, "What sort of cloth?"

"It looks like silk," said Janet. "I think," she said, straining up, "that at the back it's velvet."

Gregory looked too and it seemed the background behind the Mother was pale-brown velvet. "Velvet's terribly expensive," said Gregory, frowning.

"You would only need a little." But Gregory began to see he would need a lot. "Not of velvet. Things," he said. "Beads, sequins, gold lace. Then we have the picture to buy. We should have to buy a picture to dress up."

They stayed planning until the rain stopped and they could come out of the church to go home, Janet clutching the newspaper parcel with the lamp. They both felt warmed and cheered—until they got on the bus. When the conductress came along to take their fares, Gregory put his hand in his pocket to find his purse and his face went white. There was no purse there. He knew at once what had happened. He had put his purse, not into his shorts pocket, but into the pocket of his raincoat—the one with the hole, thought Gregory. I meant to ask Marta to mend it for me, he thought in anguish. The purse must have dropped through, in the church, on the pavement, or on the road when they ran for the bus, dropped anywhere. The conductress was holding out her hand for the money as the bus thundered along. "Come on. We'll have to get off," said Gregory but Janet, who now and then did not need to be told of calamities, put her hand in her own pocket. "You gave me back my pennies, remember," she said. As they were half-fares, Janet's pennies took them all the way home. "With one penny over," said Janet, looking at it. It did not seem much left over from thirty-five shillings. "And your threepence, my ninepence," said Janet.

44

"Shouldn't we go back to the church?" Gregory had asked. "We should be late for lunch," said Janet. "We can't tell Mother because we shouldn't have gone by ourselves." The loss of the money was the finishing touch to a dismaying morning. Janet began to cry and even Gregory had to blink back tears.

"Never mind," said Janet, though still sniffing. "We have the l-little l-lamp."

"What good is a lamp without a picture?" said Gregory.

Gregory slipped out next afternoon, although it was Sunday, and went back to the church, borrowing the fare from Marta, but though he rang the repository bell and the old woman helped him to look, there was no sign of the purse. "I'll ask Father MacGibbon," said the old woman. "Perhaps somebody gave it in to him." But no one had given it to the Father. "There are so many people on Sunday; I expect someone picked it up and put it in the poor box," she said. "The poor box or their own pocket. Dear! Dear! I am sorry."

The church was empty between Masses, and though Gregory had thought he could not bear to look at "Our Lady of Czestochowa," he did. There she was on her pillar, serene above her candles as if nothing had happened. "I can't make a picture of you now," Gregory told her. It was odd how much he minded this. "I can't make a picture. I have no money."

She stayed unmoved above the candles.

Gregory and Janet loved to make Marta tell them stories about her home, that one-roomed house in her village on the outskirts of the little town of Lutynka by the big river—"Between river and forest," said Marta. She told them about her mother, who had taught her, while she, Marta, was still a little girl, how to sew and spin and embroider and bake, as well as to cut wood and fetch water and grass and herbs for the goat. Gregory and Janet liked to hear about the goat, and the great horse Kary—which means "chestnut"—who was part of the family, and who steamed when he came with the sleigh in the snow; and about the baby piglet Marta had brought up in the kitchen. Best of all they liked to hear about the wolves. "Tell us about the wolves," they would beg.

The wolves were "a real and deadly menace," said Gregory, thrilled. Marta had a card in her workbasket, which was where, as well as the amber beads, she kept her prayer book, her Sunday earrings, and the amethyst cross her old lady had given her. The card was for Candlemass—"We don't have cards for that in England," Father said when they told him— and it showed the Virgin Mary going out in the snow, with a lighted candle to keep back a pack of wolves from a snowy village.

"We prayed that she could keep them away, because the wolves, they really come," Marta told the children. "Sometimes the whole town be cut off. Wolves stop all traffic. Wolves get on the roofs, the barn, the stable, and dig thatch up to reach horses and cows. I, in my bed, I tremble," said Marta. "I think they get Kary, but my father he make his roof walls strong, strong!" said Marta.

The landowners, Marta said, would hunt the wolves. "Make a big hunt. Twenty-two sleighs, good horse to each. Horse must be good," she would emphasize. "Good and obedient. Kary very good and obedient. Three mens on each sleigh; one to guard horse—he only have pistol—the others have guns, gun with three barrels, one for bullet, two for shots, and as well as guns, pistols, sabers"—Marta was getting excited—"and they take a bag, and in bag five or six piglet."

"Oh, no!" cried Janet, quailing.

"Not to throw to wolves," Marta assured her. "No! Only to make noise. Listen! The mens, they drive sleigh by forest, along forest edge, and pre-sent-ly," said Marta, rolling her *r*'s dramatically, "they see eyes. Eyes!"

"Wolves," whispered Gregory, pressing his hands between his knees in excitement while Janet crept nearer to Marta. "Wolves," said Marta, "and the mens, they pinch little pigs, who squeal. At once more wolves. Then slowly, slowly, each sleigh he drive further and further away, going away further from forest, and the wolves come after; two hundred wolves, five hundred, six hundred. Some packs a thousand," said Marta. "But you must know when to shoot, and, suddenly, leading man he shoot—bullet!"

The word crashed into the kitchen so that the children jumped. "Bullet. As each wolf he fall, other wolves devour," said Marta, rising up behind the kitchen table. "And now they taste blood, they come nearer, come and come. When all bullets gone and wolves are nearer, shots. Shot, shot, shot!" Marta turned on her heels, firing. "And horses they go fast. Twenty, thirty, hundred wolves fall. They stop, eat, and come on. Now so close, only pistol." Marta whipped out an imaginary pistol. "Shoot! Shoot! Shoot!" She shot the frying pan, the plate rack, the sink. "Still wolves come, close up on sleighs. Then saber. Cut! Cut! Cut!" Marta's arms whirled until she hit the saucepans with a clash that made the children leap in their chairs. "More wolves killed by saber than by shot," panted Marta. "Hundreds killed and then hunt over and sleighs gallop for home. A-aah! That is a hunt!" said Marta.

Janet had nightmares and Mother said there must be no more stories about wolves, but in daylight, Janet begged for them, "And about Kary and your mother and your little pig." But there came a day when the children could see Marta had been weeping. She scarcely spoke as she gave them their tea and they did not speak

either. It was a dark, wintry afternoon; the white and metal kitchen shone bleakly and after tea Gregory went up to his Loft.

Usually the Loft consoled him. It had been given to him by Father for his own and Father had made him a drawing table like his architect's one, with a center flap that could lift to a slant; Gregory had a T square and a case of instruments, a row of shelves for his books and paints, and a deep cupboard where he kept his collections. Above the shelves was his ship picture, a painting of a little ship plowing along in a rough sea under a pale-blue sky with cotton-wool clouds; the ship's smoke blew backward as did a scarlet pennant that streamed across the picture. Gregory loved it as he loved his watch and Rootle. They were his, but this afternoon, they and the Loft were no comfort; Gregory kept seeing Marta's face, feeling her silence. She will go away, thought Gregory, leave us and we shall have another Tove or Babette. It was not only that; he ached because Marta was unhappy. Rootle seemed to know something was wrong; he went up to Gregory, down to Marta; jumped on Gregory's table and rubbed Gregory's cheek with his crooked ear.

Janet had stayed sitting at the kitchen table; she was quite silent, which was extraordinary for Janet. At last she got up and climbed the stairs to the Loft. The door was open and she did not knock but went straight in, and for once Gregory did not order her out; in fact he did not speak at all. He was sitting at his table, in the half-dark, his feet on the rungs of the chair, his elbows on his knees, his chin on his hands, hunched and staring. Before him on the table was the little glass lamp.

Janet stood by him for some time before she said, "If you gave Marta the lamp it might cheer her up."

"A lamp's no good without a dressed-up picture." And Gregory added bitterly, "It was a fool thing to think of giving her one."

"It wasn't," said Janet, and Gregory lifted his head. He did not often let his young sister contradict him.

"It was, if I can't make it," said Gregory.

"You can make it."

"How can I make it without any money?"

"You can make it with think," said Janet.

It was not what she meant to say, yet oddly it said what she meant.

"How can you make things with *think?*" asked Gregory. He said it scornfully, but now he came to consider it, that is how things are made.

It was as if Janet had opened a little door in his mind, a door that had been shut, and once again he glimpsed the picture.

"Stupid, what should I do for silk and velvet?" he asked; though he had said "stupid," the idea had begun to grow.

"There are bits of stuff in the ragbag," said Janet. "Not those colors in the picture in the church but lots of colors, lots of scraps, and we can ask people for more."

"And gold lace for crowns?" asked Gregory. "People don't have gold lace."

"They do, but it needn't be gold. We could find a bit of white lace and paint it. There's some gold paint left over from Christmas."

"Sequins?"

"There's an old sequin evening bag in the dressing-up box. We could take a few sequins carefully off that."

"Beads?" Gregory brought each new thing out like a challenge.

Janet did not know about beads but, "I'll get some," she said.

Gregory had not unhunched himself. His spectacles glimmered in the dusk and he looked around the Loft as if he were looking for ideas. Then, "I could take my ship picture out of its frame, paint the frame, and use that," he said.

"*Your ship picture frame?*" Janet's breath was almost taken away.

"Yes, why not?"

"You mean . . . you would give it for Marta's Jesus-Mary?" asked Janet, astounded.

"The frame would look nice," said Gregory, ignoring her, "if I painted it gold." He stopped short and ducked his head again. "But it's no use."

"Why is it no use?"

"What would we do for a Jesus-Mary picture?"

Janet had not thought of that. "Could we . . . take one out of a book?"

"What book? If we took one out of Father's art books we should catch it. No, it's no good," said Gregory. "You have to have a picture before you can even start." He kicked the table leg. "It's no good. Pictures cost money and we haven't any money now."

"I've got two sixpences," offered Janet, who had two weeks' pocket money. "I spent the rest."

"We can't buy a picture for *that*," said Gregory with scorn.

There was a dismal silence until, "If you took a picture out of a newspaper you wouldn't have to buy it, would you?" asked Janet suddenly.

"Out of a *newspaper?*"

"Yes, I've just remembered. There was a big Jesus-Mary in the paper."

"In the paper?"

"Yes. In the *Times*."

"When?"

"The day before yesterday, I think. Or the day before that."

"Quick." Gregory was out of his chair. "Bet you Marta has used it for the fire, or she wrapped up something for the dustbin. Bound to," said Gregory. But Marta had not; the *Times* was there in the box in the cupboard under the stairs where old newspapers were kept. Gregory went through one after the other until he found it. He came out of the cupboard looking at the picture. Janet was right; it was a Jesus-Mary or, rather, a photograph of one. "Our Lady of the Unfad-

54

ing Flower," read out Gregory, "by Lorenzo Cosimo, late sixteenth century. This rare painting has recently been cleaned and restored and is now back on view in the Tiepolo Gallery, Milan."

"Our Lady of the Unfading Flower." Gregory carried the newspaper back to the Loft and snapped on the light as he explored the photograph. Was it big enough? Clear enough? Could it be cut out? To his eyes it was prettier than "Our Lady of Czestochowa"; the Mother was plumper, softer, wearing a long veil; the Child in her arms was laughing.

"Does it matter that he's naked?" asked Janet.

"We can make him a robe."

"He's pretty," said Janet, touching his face with her fingers. "I like him."

The flower was a tall one. "A sort of lily," said Janet; it stood at the side of the picture, "as if it were growing in the air." The picture was clear and not too small for Gregory's unaccustomed hand to dress, and the figures were easy to cut out but, "A newspaper!" said Gregory.

It was a sad comedown from his vision of jewels and glitter but, "If you stick it on cardboard and paint the faces and cover the dresses up, how will anyone know it's newspaper?" argued Janet.

"I should have to use very dry paint," said Gregory.

"You have your paints and the Christmas gold paint; we can get scraps of cloth and sequins. All you have to buy is glue, and I can lend you my sixpences for that," said Janet.

Gregory did not answer, but with his scissors he cut the picture from the newspaper, laid it on his table, and studied it again. Janet would have rushed to get some scraps and started straightaway on cutting out and sticking, but Gregory took his time. Presently he raised the center flap of his table and pinned the cutout picture on the slant, but to Janet's annoyance he went on gazing at the Madonna. At last he said, "I shall need some stiff white paper, tracing paper, and a carbon."

"Why?" asked Janet. She could not see what paper, white or tracing, and carbons had to do with sticking on robes and crowns. "Why?"

"Don't talk so much. Go and get them," was all Gregory would say.

Janet was used to being transformed into an office boy; she found the tracing paper and drawing pins on Gregory's shelves, and while he pinned a sheet of tracing paper over the picture she went downstairs to find the stiff white paper.

"Is this stiff enough?" she asked when she came back. "It's a bit of Mother's cartridge paper. She let me have it. But why do you want it? Why?"

"Quiet," growled Gregory.

It was not easy to trace the dark newspaper photograph, but slowly, inch by inch, Gregory succeeded in finding the outlines of the two figures, of their faces and hands, of veil and robes and hair, while Janet watched, fascinated. Once again Gregory did not order her out; he only said, "Don't breathe down my neck."

Soon she was sent for the typewriter carbon. There were plenty in Father's and Mother's workrooms. "An old one will do if it's not too smudgy," said Gregory. Janet found one in the wastepaper basket; fortunately no one had crinkled it up, and when she brought it, Gregory lifted the picture to one side, then carefully pinned the stiff white paper, the carbon, and the tracing paper onto the board and went over his traced lines with a thick pencil. When he lifted the tracing and carbon away, there, to Janet's admiration, was the picture's outline in thick blue lines on the white paper— Mother, Child, veil, cloak and all. "But they haven't crowns," said Janet. "We'll make them crowns," said Gregory. He studied the blue and white shapes, then slowly, meticulously, began to cut them up. "Cut them up?" asked Janet, bewildered. "Why?" But Gregory did not answer, only continued to cut: the shape of the background, of the Mother; then he cut off the outlines of her veil and her cloak and, around the Child's figure, cut a flat stiff robe. They fitted together on the table like pieces of a puzzle.

"But what are they *for?*" asked Janet, and this time Gregory did answer. "They are my templates," he said.

"Templates?"

"Like Father makes when he wants a pattern: sizes and shapes of what I shall need. You see, we shall have to try pieces of cloth over and over again. These will make their shapes. Now I need a piece of cardboard," said Gregory, "to fit the frame."

"Use the cardboard at the back of the ship picture," suggested Janet—it was accepted by both of them that the ship picture was to be used, sacrificed for its frame—but it was bedtime before they could do any more.

Next day the next-door children came to tea—"Bother," said Gregory—and the next Mother took him to the dentist; it was not until Saturday that Gregory was able to do what he had longed to do all the week—go back to the Loft and work on the Madonna.

To get the ship painting out of the frame was not difficult; it was sealed with brown paper and held by small pin nails which Gregory kept. "We shall want them when we put the new picture in." But when the Madonna was laid on the cardboard she did not fit it; the newspaper picture was smaller than the frame by more than an inch each way. "What will you do about that?" asked Janet.

"Make a border," said Gregory. He said it without thinking, then saw that it was exactly what he would have to do. "A border of what?" asked Janet, but Gregory pushed that thought aside. He had enough to think of now and he wished Janet would not ask questions; he wanted to be more and more silent as he grew more and more interested. He had cut an oblong of the stiff white paper the same size as the cardboard and pinned this new sheet to the slant of his table; it was on this oblong that he would build up his picture; the newspaper one he pinned beside him on the flat. Janet still breathed down his neck as he worked but something seemed to stop Gregory from snapping at her; perhaps it was those two pairs of pictured eyes that looked so steadily at him. He was patient with Janet and let her stay where she had never been allowed to stay before, in the Loft. He even let her go on with her questions.

"What will you do about the hands?"

"Cut them out and stick them over the clothes."

"Will you give them hair? Real hair?"

"I don't know," said Gregory.

"What will you . . .?" But Gregory, for the moment, had finished. "Come and look for pieces of cloth," he said.

The right pieces were difficult to find. Gregory was fussy but it seemed the picture was more fussy, because everything they tried somehow did not fit. Gregory went through the ragbag but there were no bits of silk or velvet or brocade; the nearest was some green velveteen from Janet's party frock; the rest were scraps of striped flannel from old pajamas, pieces of linen from worn-out pillowcases or handkerchiefs, colored cottons from summer dresses. "All so ordinary," Gregory said disgustedly.

"We're an ordinary family," said Janet. She was getting tired of Gregory's fussiness and besides, to her, the green velveteen would have done perfectly well for the cloak, with a pretty piece of pink cotton for the Baby. "You want scraps from queens and princesses," she said indignantly and stopped. "Greg, there *is* a princess who buys her hats from Madame Ginette."

"Madame Ginette?"

"You know, who makes Mother's hats. She's always telling Mother about her precious princess. She bought this, she tried on that . . . ." Janet mimicked an old Frenchwoman. "The princess ordered ten hats when she went to America."

"Well?" asked Gregory, as if to say, What is this to do with the picture?

"Once, when I went with Mother, Madame Ginette gave me a piece of ribbon, all embroidered with roses. She said it was for my dolls. Her shop is only in the Crescent. She might give us scraps."

"Go and ask her," commanded Gregory.

"I wouldn't dare," said Janet. "She's frightening, like an old witch. Besides, today's Saturday. She's shut."

"And she'll be shut tomorrow, Sunday. Two whole days to wait," said Gregory. "You must ask her on Monday."

"I can't. It's dancing class afternoon," said Janet, hedging.

"Pestering nuisance," Gregory grumbled.

"I can't help it." Then Janet swallowed and said, "If you'll come with me, I'll ask her, but you'll have to wait till Tuesday."

By Monday afternoon though, Gregory felt he could not wait. All the weekend he had had visions of princesses' hats in gold and silver and pearls, and when Janet had come back from school, and then, escorted by Marta, with her dancing shoes and hairbrush in a case, had gone to her class, Gregory went up to his bedroom. To make hats for a princess sounded a little like being a court jeweler and he would not risk making the same mistake twice. He washed his hands, scrubbed his nails, and going into Father's dressing room, slicked down his hair with Father's hair cream. He put on fresh socks and pulled them up with his garters, turning them neatly down, and polished his best walking shoes until they shone. Then he folded his school muffler under his new overcoat and brushed his cap.

"No, Rootle, I'm not going to the Gardens. Stay here," he said as Rootle rubbed against his legs, asking to come, and Gregory let himself out the front door.

At the end of the Crescent was a little row of shops, not like the shops in the High Street, but smaller and obviously more expensive: a shop with old china; an upholsterer's shop that had a brocaded chair and a wheel-barrow filled with flowers in the window; a furrier's that had nothing at all but a fashion paper and a sign; and next door, Madame Ginette's. Gregory's step grew slower and slower. To go into any shop was bad; to go into a woman's shop was dreadful.

In the window were two hats; one, in black with feathers, Gregory dismissed, but the other was blue on a gold model. If I had a bit of that blue, thought Gregory. Blue and gold, he felt, were his colors. Madame Ginette had given Janet a ribbon; Gregory drew a deep breath and went in.

The door had a jangling bell, rather like the shabby

shops off the High Street, and as Gregory set it jangling, a dark little old woman appeared in the shop so quickly that she might have been a cork popped from a bottle. It was a tiny room, in white and moss green, and it was lined with mirrors and filled with hats. Gregory felt more and more of an interloper; what was a schoolboy doing here? Then Madame Ginette came nearer and he smelled a familiar smell. Madame had been eating onions, like Marta, and she had been smoking a cigarette; at once the little shop felt more homely. Nor did Madame Ginette look grand, not at all like the lordly men in Rostov's, and not at all like someone who made hats for a princess, Gregory thought. She was dressed in black with a darned black cardigan, wore felt slippers, and her stockings were wrinkled; on her black waist apron dangled a pincushion stuck with pins. She was also wearing a thimble.

"A very unexpected customer," she said, only she said *vairy*.

"I'm not a customer," said Gregory. He had taken off his cap and was scarlet to his ears.

"Then?"

"I am Gregory Thomas. You make hats for my mother."

"Ah! The dear Mrs. Thomas. You have a message for me? Yes?"

"No," said Gregory. He did not seem able to get any further, but stood twisting his cap helplessly. "I . . . I . . . ." Then, "Madame," he burst out, "would you,

64

could you, give me some bits and pieces of material left over from your princess's hats?"

"My princess? Why the princess?" Gregory could not answer and Madame Ginette asked, "Do you like her so much?"

"I don't know her," said Gregory.

"Then why?"

"I need," said Gregory, suddenly finding his tongue and his coaxing flute voice, "I need some beautiful, wonderful scraps."

"Some beautiful, wonderful scraps?"

Perhaps the vision of splendor that Gregory so plainly saw touched the old Frenchwoman because her voice was gentle as she said, "But, *mon petit*, the princess's hats are the same as anybody else's; the same as your mother's," only she said *mozzer's*.

"No," said Gregory unbelievingly.

"But yes. That black one in the window is for her."

Black! It was another dream exploded. Gregory managed to say, "I . . . I'm sorry I bothered you. Goodby," as he went toward the door, but Madame Ginette stopped him. "That does not mean I do not have beautiful scraps, but you must tell me for what you want them; tell me exactly," only she said *ezactly*. "You, a boy, do not make doll clothes, no?"

"No!" said Gregory with such repugnance that she laughed. Gregory looked up at her and said, "I should have to know first that you can keep a secret."

Madame Ginette lifted a finger, spat on it, and drew

it across her throat. For the first time Gregory smiled and then he, who never, as Mother complained, told anyone anything, told Madame Ginette about Marta, the good place, and the Kitchen Madonna.

"Great heavens, gracious me!" said Janet. She had come back with Marta and climbed up to the Loft to tell Gregory to come down for tea. "Heavens! Gracious me!"

On Gregory's table was a heap of scraps: velvet and silk and taffeta and muslin; bits of ribbon and cord, gold thread and embroidery silk; colored glass beads, odds and ends of flowers and lace. "*Where* did you get them?"

"From Madame Ginette."

"But . . . did *you* go to Madame Ginette?"

"Obviously," said Gregory.

"You . . . went . . . to . . . Madame Ginette's *alone?*" Janet surveyed this astonishingly changed brother.

"Why not?"

"You *spoke* to her?"

"How else would I get the scraps?"

"But . . . wasn't she frightening?"

"Not at all. I like her."

"But you don't like people."

"I like Madame Ginette. She's a nice old bird," said Gregory carelessly.

"Old bir . . . ." Janet's voice failed her.

"I have promised to show her the picture when it is finished," said Gregory.

Among the scraps was a piece of blue ribbon. Blue again, thought Gregory, and, "This *is* beautiful," Madame Ginette had said. "See the true deep-blue, royal-blue you call it. I have trimmed a hat of this . . . no, not for the princess, but a royal hat."

Royal-blue seemed right for a queenly cloak and there were snippets of lace that, painted gold, would make the crowns.

"Now you can get on," said Janet, but Gregory still pieced colors together, trying them against the Madonna's face and hands, then discarding them. "*When* are you going to find something that will *do?*" Janet asked, exasperated.

"It mustn't *do*. It must be right." He was so slow that Janet almost lost interest. "You've had her more than a week and not a single thing is stuck."

Gregory did not tell Janet, but his difficulty was the background. I want it to look like the sky, he told himself over and over again, but nothing looked like the sky. Janet brought a square of pale-blue velvet she had traded for at school. "I gave a pencil sharpener for it, and a whole packet of peppermints," she said and, as if she had caught Gregory's thought, added, "It is the color of the sky." But when the velvet was cut out by its template and laid around the Madonna, it did not look at all like the sky; it looked like a piece of velvet, throwing back the light, and it was far too thick. Janet almost cried with disappointment.

"That comes of using a newspaper picture," said Gregory.

"Perhaps you ought to use paper," said Janet and, "I know where there's a sky," she said.

"Where?"

"In your ship picture."

It was Gregory's turn to have his breath taken away. "My ship picture?"

"It's a beautiful sky and nice crisp paper," said Janet calmly. "And the picture's not much use without the frame, is it? You might as well cut it up." But Gregory was shocked.

"Cut up my ship picture for Marta?"

"Well, you have given her the frame," Janet pointed out.

When Janet had gone, Gregory looked at his ship picture. He looked at it for a long time, then pinned it on his board and drew the shape of the background template on the best bit of the sky, right across the cotton-wool clouds. He picked up the scissors. There was a pang when he saw the little steamer fall away onto the table, its pennant severed, but, "This is a more important picture," he told Rootle, who had come upstairs. Rootle had a way of knowing when Gregory was troubled, and he wrapped his tail around his paws as he sat, and blinked at Gregory as if he understood. When Gregory had cut the sky to the template and fitted it around the Mother and Child, the pale-blue painted sky with its clouds looked exactly right; they gave depth to the whole picture. It was the first right step and almost at once he found the next; he and Janet had emptied Madame Ginette's scraps into an old carton so that they could turn them over and over. "And stop Rootle playing with them," said Gregory—the scraps seemed to have made Rootle behave like a kitten again. Now, as Gregory turned them over, spilling half of them on the floor, he found a piece of coral-colored cotton that, he suddenly saw, would make the veil and the Baby's robe. He laid it beside Madame Ginette's royal-blue ribbon and again it looked right: the blue of the Mother's robe, the coral for the Child and the veil. Gregory drew a breath of satisfaction. He had begun.

There were never any hours more peaceful than those Gregory spent with the Madonna in his Loft. As he worked, her eyes seemed to dwell on him, encouraging him, as did the Child's. Marta said they looked at you, thought Gregory, and she was right. He ran up to the Loft directly after he had had his tea and nowadays he hardly ever asked his question, "Is Mother in?" In fact it was the other way about: "What *is* Gregory doing?" asked Mother. "We never see him nowadays."

"Hush," said Janet, and Mother hushed.

Janet got tired of the picture and went to play next

door. "I can't work at that Madonna for *ever*," she said, but Rootle often took her place. When he wanted attention Rootle had a way of sitting down on anything Gregory was working on, but he never sat on the picture that was growing, nor on the newspaper one. It was as if he knew he must respect them and he would sit in his neat way, tail around paws, on the far side of the table, watching Gregory's hands. Only now and then would he put out a paw and dab at a scrap.

Even when Gregory was away from the picture, he carried it in his mind; he thought about it in bed and at meals, on his walks, even at school. "Gregory isn't paying quite the attention he used to," his master told Father. "Nothing to worry about, in fact the reverse. He was a bit too much on pins and needles," and, "Gregory, I think you're getting fatter," said Mother one morning at breakfast.

Though it was peaceful, the work was intricate and fiddling and Gregory often felt his hands were all thumbs, though to Janet he seemed wonderfully deft. There was an anxious moment when the faces were cut from the newspaper picture and glued in position on the white, and he was ready to put on the cloak and the Baby's robe and the veil. The shapes of the cotton and ribbon, when they were cut out, curled at the edges; they would curl worse when they were glued. "Iron them," suggested Janet.

"How can I when they are glued?" said Gregory, worried.

The first cutouts he made had to be thrown away; fortunately there was more muslin, but the royal-blue ribbon was ruined and Gregory had to substitute a piece of blue cotton to make the robe. "It's not nearly as lovely," he mourned, but this picture had a way of making things right; the cotton was not Madame Ginette's exquisite royal-blue, but oddly enough, its dullness looked better; as if the Madonna knew she was destined for the kitchen and preferred the simpler cloths. In the end Gregory had to treat the pieces like pressed flowers, pressing them down under blotting paper and weights and then spreading glue quickly, and quickly putting them in place.

When the robes and veil were on, Gregory painted the folds in Chinese white, copying from those in the newspaper picture. Then he painted the newspaper faces and hands, mixing his paint to a rosy peach; to his surprise the paint took well on the paper. When he came to the eyes his hand trembled so much that he decided to leave them alone. "I don't want to spoil the way they have of looking," he told Janet, but with a mapping pen and brown paint, he drew in the eyebrows and lash lines and, with thicker paint, made lines for the hair.

"Wouldn't you like some real hair, doll's hair, to stick on?" asked Janet; she was longing for him to use real hair and brought two of her dolls up to the Loft ready to sacrifice their wigs. But Gregory only took a lock of brown hair from one of them and teased it into wisps, curling them lightly on the Baby's head. Janet's dolls were useful; one of her girl dolls had a necklace of a gold chain linked by pearls and yellow beads; the yellow ones looked like Marta's amber.

As Gregory worked he could see the picture growing under his hands, the figures beginning to stand out, and an answering pride and warmth seemed to inspire him. The halos behind the heads he painted in gilt—"They're only a background for the crowns." Before he made the crowns he disobeyed again—"I have to," said Gregory—and went back to the church to have another look at "Our Lady of Czestochowa." He stayed so long gazing at her that two or three people paused, as if they were struck by what they thought was a small boy's devotion but, "My Madonna is prettier than you," Gregory was telling the picture and, "I wonder if I can make my crowns look as good as that?"

He shaped them from an inch or two of Madame Ginette's lace and gilded them, then glued them onto the heads over the golden halos. At first he thought the crowns stood out too much—"And the Baby's is a bit crooked," Gregory told Rootle, annoyed—but no, they made the picture more alive.

Now the anxious part was over it was fun; onto points of glue put on with a pin, Gregory dropped the pearls and beads with Mother's eyebrow tweezers until the veil and the Child's robe were beaded, the Child's robe more stiffly—"Covered with beads," said Janet.

Gregory let her drop some, and even let her put one or two glass beads on the crowns. As a finishing touch, he took the gold chain that had been the doll's necklace, cut it to the right length with his tweezers, then delicately drew it through a dab of glue held in Janet's palm, and edged the Mother's halo with it. "It looks splendid," cried Janet.

For the flower that gave the picture its name, "Our Lady of the Unfading Flower," he did not choose one of Madame Ginette's flowers; they looked wrong, too heavy and pale; he tried a Japanese water flower, drying it carefully when it had opened out, but laid on the picture it seemed to stand out too much. In the end, his tongue held anxiously in his teeth, Gregory copied it—"I can't really paint, you know"—but its shape and the faint-pink of water flowers seemed right and, "It doesn't look too grown-up for us or for Marta," said Janet. Then, "What will you use for the border?" she asked.

It took Gregory a long time to think of the border, and when it came, it came "by accident," he might have said. He had tried braid, bits of ribbon, and strips of cloth to fill the gap between the picture and the frame, but nothing looked right until, to help him in his solitude, Janet brought him a bag of toffees. Among the gaudy papers they were wrapped in were a few metal papers, shining in jewel colors; there was a green for emerald, a dark sapphire-blue, a gold, and a magenta pink—though no jewel Gregory knew had that startling color. Unwrapped and smoothed out, the papers lost their creases, and cut in half, they filled the depth of the border space. Laid one beside the next they made a shining checkered edge. These are what I shall use, thought Gregory, but this brought a problem. "Money again," Gregory told Rootle, and sighed.

"There are four metal-wrapped toffees in this quarter of a pound; that gives me eight pieces of paper if I cut them in half," said Gregory. Rootle listened attentively. "I need eight at the top and eight at the bottom of the picture, twelve along the sides. That's another pound of toffees, *presuming*," said Gregory, "presuming I get four metal-wrapped toffees to each quarter. Janet paid one shilling and threepence for that quarter, so that a pound of toffees will cost five shillings." But he did not have five shillings, and thinking of his lost purse and the stopping of his pocket money, Gregory gave a great sigh.

He went to the sweetshop. What made him decide to carry out this business, too, without Janet he did not know, but he went alone and stood studying the toffees in their big glass scoop. As well as green, blue, and pink metal-wrapped ones there were some red—rubies, thought Gregory—and purple ones like amethysts. He stayed, looking at them, until the sweetshop woman said, "Yes, dear?"

Gregory and Janet knew her well, though Gregory did not know her name; with Janet she was firm friends, but Gregory had never spoken to her. She always gave Janet one or two extra sweets and now and again a lollipop, but she weighed out Gregory's quarter pounds or gave him a Mars bar or slab of chocolate without speaking. She was a big woman; her blue apron bulged as she stood behind the counter and her arms were—like bolsters, thought Gregory. Her chestnut hair was piled up in puffs and combs and when she smiled, though it was a friendly smile, she showed big white teeth. Gregory almost went away to fetch Janet but, "Yes, dear? What is it you want?" the sweetshop woman was saying.

Gregory took a deep gulp and went up to the counter, where he slowly unstrapped his watch; he was glad the shop was empty. "May I speak to you?" asked Gregory and he laid his watch down on the counter. "This is my birthday watch," he said. "It's silver, with fifteen jewels, waterproof. You can take it swimming and it won't hurt."

"Yes, dear," said the sweetshop woman as if she were wondering why she was being told all this.

"Could I leave it with you as a hostage?" asked Gregory. He was not sure he had the right word. "A hostage for a pound of those toffees."

"But . . . *dear!*" said the woman, her whole attention caught. "Dear! This watch is worth far more than a pound of toffees."

"Yes, that's why I thought you would let me have them," said Gregory.

77

"But *dear!*" said the sweetshop woman again. "I'm sure your mother wouldn't like it."

"Mother's out," said Gregory. And he continued rapidly, "Even if she was in I couldn't ask her. I can't ask her because she would want to know why Janet and I haven't any money and then she would have to know—everything—and I can't tell her for reasons . . ." said Gregory, tailing off.

"We do get money, of course," he went on. "Our pocket money on Saturdays. Mine was stopped for two weeks but now it has started again and I can always use Janet's. That's why I know I can pay you back, but this week I need some more glue and another decent brush and I had to pay a bus fare, so it might be some time . . . ." And before Gregory knew it, just as he had told Madame Ginette, he told the sweetshop woman all about Marta and the good place and the Kitchen Madonna.

"Well, knock me flat!" said the sweetshop woman when he had finished. "Who would ever have thought you were that kind of a boy. Proper stuck-up I thought you were; never a word for anybody. Not like your little sister at all, and now. . . . Well, I never!" There was a pause in which she seemed to be making up her mind. "But I can't take your watch, dearie. It wouldn't be right." And she handed it back to Gregory.

"*Please*, please, I would make it right," said Gregory, using his coaxing flute voice, but she shook her head.

"No, love, it wouldn't be right. But I'll tell you what I'll do. I'll take your I.O.U."

"My I.O.U.?"

"That's right. Look, I'll write on this paper, 'I.O.U. 4/8½d one pound of toffees'—that's what they are by the pound—and you sign and put your address and then you pay me back as soon as you can. Could you pay me sixpence every Saturday?"

"Yes, I could," said Gregory.

"Right. I'll make it out like that and when you've paid it up, I give the paper back to you."

"Oh, thank you! Thank you, Mrs. . . . ." Gregory wished he knew her name.

"Mrs. Bartholomew's the name," said the sweetshop woman. "But they call me Barty."

"Thank you, Barty," said Gregory and then, as she began to weigh the toffees out, he said anxiously, "Could you make sure that a . . . ." He did not know quite how to put it, and then two unusual words came to him. unusual even for Gregory. "Could you make sure that a goodly proportion of those shiny jewelly-paper ones go in?"

The woman glanced at Gregory, and perhaps those funny old-fashioned words or the earnestness of his face touched her, as Madame Ginette had been touched— "Though goodness knows I'm used to kids," she would have said—and, picking them out especially, she put in two whole handfuls of the jewel-wrapped toffees, enough to cover the back of the picture as well. Then, "Do you think," she said, like a child herself, "when this wonder of a picture is finished, you could bring it and show it to me?"

There came a day when the last sequin and bead had been dropped into place—"and stuck, thank goodness," said Gregory—the last square of toffee paper filled into the border. Gregory put the picture into the newly painted frame, backed it with the cardboard, and taking care not to shake it in case any beads came off, he gently hammered the pin nails in again with Father's smallest hammer. When he had knocked them flat, he covered the join between cardboard and frame with brown-paper sealing strips as it had been covered before. Then he made a patchwork of toffee papers so that "The back looks almost as nice as the front," said Janet. For a finishing touch, in his best script Gregory wrote a label with the picture's name: *Our Lady of the Unfading Flower, by Lorenzo Cosimo,* but underneath he wrote, *A Kitchen Madonna for Marta.*

"You are invited," said Janet at the drawing-room door, "to a private view in Gregory's Loft, to see what he has made."

"Gregory has *made* something?" asked Mother as if

she did not believe it, and Father put down his spectacles. "Made something?"

"Yes." Janet looked unusually clean and tidy but now she became Janet again. "Don't be cross with him for being disobedient," she pleaded. "And don't, don't ask him where his ship picture has gone."

The Loft had been swept and tidied; the carton of scraps pushed into the cupboard, the snippets and bits of silver and paper that had littered the floor, gathered up. The paint and glue were on their shelf, the brushes standing in a jar of turpentine. It was Gregory's tidy way, though Janet had grown impatient. "Why?" she had asked.

"We want them to look at the picture," said Gregory, "not bother about the Loft."

The picture lay on the slanted table; its colors and sequins flashed under the electric light; the Madonna's eyes looked out in their quiet way while the Child seemed to smile. When Mother and Father came in they stood and gazed and gazed until, "Gregory made *that?*" asked Mother.

"All out of his own head," said Janet. "Every little bit himself."

"You helped a lot," said Gregory.

"But it's your picture," said Janet. "Listen! Listen, Mother." And the story came tumbling out, Janet telling first, Gregory interrupting. They told it from the beginning: Marta's unhappiness, the British Museum, Fabergé and his fine example, the young man in the shop. "Rostov's—whew!" said Father, and Gregory winced again as he remembered it. "I'm sorry, Dad," he said. "But you see I had to go." Janet had already gone on to the rain that drove them into the church and was telling about the church shop and the lamp and the picture on the pillar. "Our Lady of C-Z-E-S-T-O-C-H-O-W-A." Gregory had to spell it out to them. He did not know how to pronounce it. "That must be a copy of the famous picture," said Mother. "It's in Poland."

"It said, 'Queen of Poland,' " said Janet.

When they came to the loss of the money, Mother might have said, "That comes of disobeying," but she did not. "Because of Janet," said Gregory—and Janet glowed with pleasure—"because of Janet I found a way to make the picture after all."

Rootle had come up too and took his station on the table. He was purring while Mother sat down to look at the picture, poring over it. Now that she looked at it closely she could see it might have been made by a boy: the Child's crown was slightly crooked, one of the Madonna's cheeks had run, two of the edging papers were out of line, but, "Made by a boy with imagination and love," said Mother, reaching for Father's hand. "Oh, Gregory! Gregory!" And she burst into tears.

Janet stopped talking at once. The stiffness came back into Gregory. "But I didn't do anything wrong," he said. "Except when we went to Rostov's shop and when I went back to the church. It's only a Kitchen Madonna,"

said Gregory, getting more worried. "All made out of nothing. I didn't spend anything: only Janet's pocket money for glue and paint, and the toffees of course, but I'll pay that back soon." He could not think of anything he had done that was so very wrong, except his disobedience—but *they haven't scolded me for that,* thought Gregory. "Why are you so miserable? What have I *done?*" he asked almost in a wail.

"What have you done?" said Mother through her tears. "Lots of things. You began by sharing Rootle with Marta. You gave up your ship picture. You were ready to give up your watch, and here we all are in your Loft where you would never let us in."

"I come in and out all the time now," Janet boasted.

"Yes!" said Mother. "You let us in, Greg, and you have come out," said Mother, which they did not understand. "I'm not crying because I'm miserable," said Mother. "I'm crying because I'm happy." And she put her arm around Gregory and held him close as if he were Janet—and, Gregory "allowed her to," said Janet.

"Why didn't you light the little light for them to see it all complete?" asked Janet afterward, but Gregory shook his head. "The first one to light that light must be Marta."

It was decided to wait until after tea on Saturday when all the family were in. "Then we can all share it," said Mother.

She inveigled Marta upstairs by pretending she wanted to go through the linen cupboard, and when they were out of the way, Father, Gregory, and Janet tiptoed into the kitchen.

Gregory knew where the good place should be—where Marta had pointed when she had told them of the good place in her home. In the angle of the wall was a small shelf on which the coffee pot always stood. "But it can stand somewhere else," Gregory had said and Mother had agreed. Now he and Janet washed the white paint of the shelf and put a length of red velvet along it—Mother had found it—and on the velvet laid a mat of crocheted white lace which she had cut and sewn for them to the shelf's shape. "Marta will like the red showing through the lace," she said. At the right height on the wall Father hung the picture so that its lower edge was three inches above the shelf. Janet filled a miniature silver vase that Mother had given them with snowdrops and stood it to one side. In front of the picture was the little red lamp, its wick ready. Gregory put a box of matches on the table. "Now!" Janet called to Mother.

"Marta," said Mother, putting down the sheet she was holding. "Marta, I hear you are sad in our kitchen because there is no good place."

"*Maty Bozha!* Mother of God!" Marta's pale face flamed crimson. "The children! They tell you. Ah! They should not have said!"

"They would not have said it if there was no good

place now," said Mother, putting her hand on Marta's arm. "At least we hope it is a good place. Gregory made it for you. Don't be cross with them. Come and see." She turned Marta toward the stairs. "Come and see."

Mother had wept when she saw the picture—"Though I still don't know why," said Janet—but when Marta saw the good place, she stood quite still. Then slowly she lifted her hands and her whole face was transformed. "*Maty Bozha!*" breathed Marta, but in a very different way from the way she had said it upstairs. She took one step nearer. "*Matir Bozha!*" she breathed again, and then she began to speak. None of them could understand the words she said, but even Janet knew it was a prayer or a hymn of thanksgiving and praise. It was loud, ringing, so loud that Rootle got up out of his basket and came first to Marta and then to Gregory and rubbed himself against their legs, adding his purring to Marta's praise. The strange words filled the kitchen: "*Maty Bozha zmylujsia nad namy . . .*" and, though he could not understand one of them, they seemed to go deep into Gregory, thrilling him so that he tingled. When the prayer was finished Marta broke into laughter, happy, exulting laughter. "Now Marta never unhappy, never no more!" She threw her arms around each of them in turn and kissed them, even Father.

It was quite a time before the kitchen was quiet enough for Mother to tell Marta the history of the Madonna. "You mustn't thank us," said Mother, and Marta's eyes did have tears in them as the story was told again, and she looked at Gregory much as she had looked at the picture, in wonder and thanksgiving. When Mother had finished, Marta went up to him; for a moment Gregory wondered what she was going to do—he had shrunk a little under those exuberant kisses—but Marta only put out her hand and took his. Then very gravely she shook it, "As if I were a grown-up gentleman," said Gregory.

It was not until Marta was alone with the children that she lit the lamp. "My little litted lamp," said Marta, and when she did it there was an unexpected beauty, something extra, like a gift. Under the electric lights of the Loft and kitchen, the picture had scintillated and shone, but in the softer glow of the lamp it changed and now Gregory saw why these pictures were made with cloth; their richness of color sprang into life but the folds and edges were shadowed, making the figures look alive. Here and there a sequin shone like a jewel, the silver sparkled softly, the crowns were rich, the whole picture was bathed in gold, and the eyes looked and looked.

"Gregory," Janet called from her room when they were in bed. "Gregory, you know what? I think your picture's better than the ones in the Museum."

"Don't be an idiot," said Gregory, but he was pleased.

"It is, and *much* better than the four hundred and thirty-eight guineas one in the jewel shop!"

"Don't be a silly idiot," said Gregory, but he was more pleased.

"Gregory," she called a little later as if she had been thinking. "Gregory, what will you make now?"

"I think I shall make a picture for Madame Ginette," said Gregory. "A hat shop Madonna. And I shall make one for Barty."

"Do you call Mrs. Bartholomew—*Barty*?" asked Janet.

"Yes, she's my friend," said Gregory absently. "She would like a sweetshop Madonna; we could make it out of the wrappings of all kinds of different sweets. I might make one for Mother but, heck, she mustn't cry. I shall make dozens of Madonnas," said Gregory, lying on his back, Rootle curled up against him. "Better and better Madonnas, more and more beautiful. Probably some day some of them will go in the Museum. Rostov's might sell them." And Gregory saw Mr. Needham bowing low to him. "I might be as famous as Fabergé," said Gregory with a yawn and he turned over on his side to dream. . . .